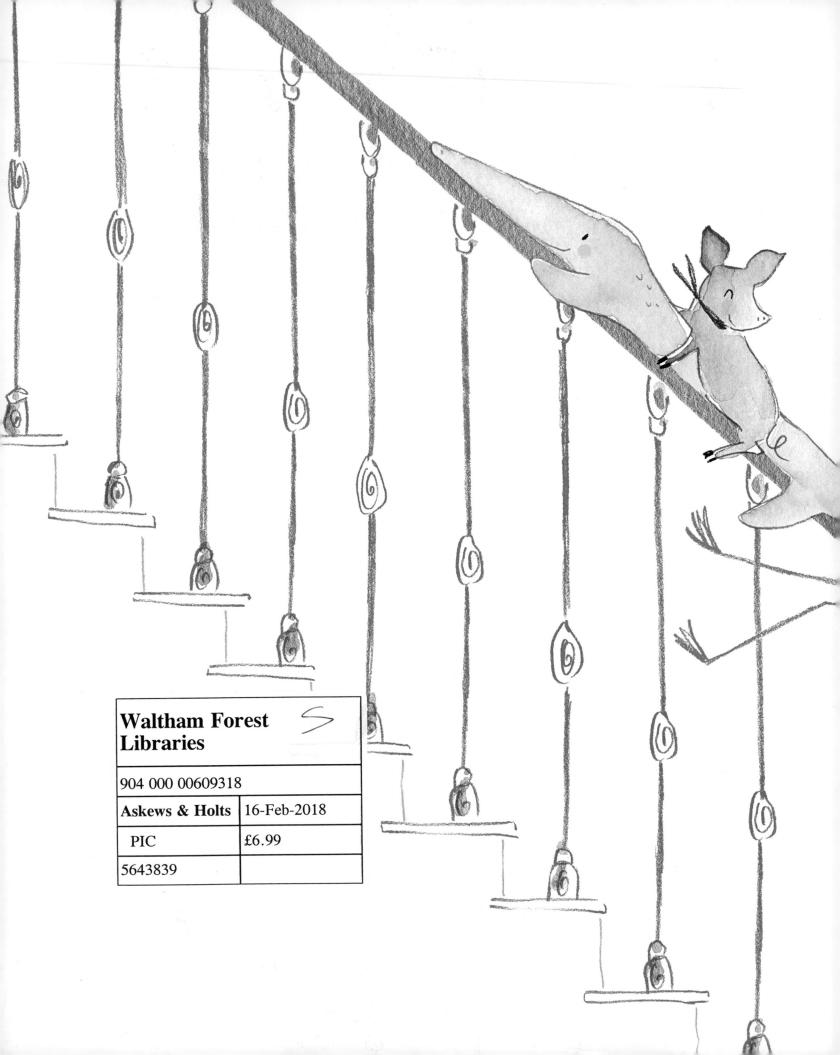

Lola Dutch
is a Little Bit Much

Kenneth &
Sarah Jane
Wright

BLOOMSBURY
LONDON OXFORD NEW YORK NEW DELHI SYDNEY

This is Lola. Lola Dutch.

Lola Dutch is a little bit much.

"Good morning, Bear!" said Lola.
"Today is going to be AMAZING!
I'm just BURSTING with ideas!"
  "Goodness," said Bear. "First, might
we start the day with tea and toast?"

  "Oh no, I have grander ideas for breakfast," said Lola.
"Come, Bear, the kitchen awaits!"

Bear took a deep breath. Lola's ideas could be a bit much.

Croc wanted crumpets.
"What's crumpets without
syrup?" asked Lola.

Pig wanted pastries.
"And hot chocolate with
marshmallows, of course!"

Crane wanted crêpes.
"One can never have
too much whipped
cream."

Bear braced himself.

"Lola Dutch, you are a little bit much," said Bear.

On their morning walk, Lola had another grand idea.
"Bear, I feel like a little light reading."

At the library, Croc studied the great inventors.

Pig observed the great chemists.

Crane researched the great writers.

Lola discovered the
great artists, and her
imagination ran . . .

...wild.

As did her library card.

"Lola Dutch, this is just so much!" said Bear.

"Oh, Bear," said Lola, "I'm still BURSTING with ideas! When we get home, it's time to PAINT!"

Croc collected the brushes.

Pig mixed the paint.

Crane gathered the canvas.

"As the great artist Matisse said, 'Creativity takes courage!'
Forward, friends!"

et voilà !

Bear smiled. "Lola Dutch, you are just too much."

"Thank you, Bear. Next, I need to . . ."
"Oh no, that's enough!" said Bear. "It's bedtime."

"All right," said Lola. "But first
I need a bubble bath,

my favourite pyjamas

and a bedtime story."

Bear was very much
ready for bedtime.

Still, Lola felt one more
burst of creativity.

"Tonight I think we should sleep in something a bit more majestic," said Lola.

But Croc had cold feet. Pig snorted and snored.
Crane kicked in her sleep.

"This is ALL TOO MUCH!"

said Lola Dutch.